PLEASE RETURN TO

THANK YOU

Made in the USA
Monee, IL
22 August 2021

76292628R00068